D0464040

Dear Parent:
Your child's love of reading starts here!

Every child learns to read in a different way and at his or her own speed. Some go back and forth between reading levels and read favorite books again and again. Others read through each level in order. You can help your young reader improve and become more confident by encouraging his or her own interests and abilities. From books your child reads with you to the first books he or she reads alone, there are I Can Read Books for every stage of reading:

SHARED READING
Basic language, word repetition, and whimsical illustrations, ideal for sharing with your emergent reader

BEGINNING READING
Short sentences, familiar words, and simple concepts for children eager to read on their own

READING WITH HELP
Engaging stories, longer sentences, and language play for developing readers

READING ALONE
Complex plots, challenging vocabulary, and high-interest topics for the independent reader

ADVANCED READING
Short paragraphs, chapters, and exciting themes for the perfect bridge to chapter books

I Can Read Books have introduced children to the joy of reading since 1957. Featuring award-winning authors and illustrators and a fabulous cast of beloved characters, I Can Read Books set the standard for beginning readers.

A lifetime of discovery begins with the magical words **"I Can Read!"**

Visit www.icanread.com for information on enriching your child's reading experience.

I Can Read Book® is a trademark of HarperCollins Publishers.

Superman Classic: Superman versus the Silver Banshee
Copyright © 2013 DC Comics.
SUPERMAN and all related characters and elements are trademarks of and © DC Comics.
(s13)

HARP2642
Manufactured in China. No part of this book may be used or reproduced in any manner whatsoever without written permission except in the case of brief quotations embodied in critical articles and reviews. For information address HarperCollins Children's Books, a division of HarperCollins Publishers, 10 East 53rd Street, New York, NY 10022.
www.harpercollinschildrens.com

Library of Congress catalog card number: 2012936203
ISBN 978-0-06-188524-2

Book design by John Sazaklis

12 13 14 15 16   SCP   10 9 8 7 6 5 4 3 2 1   ❖   First Edition

I Can Read!™

READING WITH HELP 2

SUPERMAN™

versus the Silver Banshee

by Donald Lemke
pictures by Andy Smith

SUPERMAN created by Jerry Siegel and Joe Shuster

HARPER

An Imprint of HarperCollinsPublishers

CLARK KENT

Clark Kent is a
newspaper reporter.
He is secretly Superman.

LOIS LANE

Lois Lane is a
reporter. She works
for the *Daily Planet*
newspaper.

SUPERMAN

Superman has
many amazing powers.
He was born on the planet
Krypton.

LEX LUTHOR

Lex Luthor is a wealthy Metropolis businessman. He is Superman's enemy.

SILVER BANSHEE

Silver Banshee is the daughter of a powerful Gaelic clan leader. An evil witch gave her magic superpowers.

S.T.A.R. LABS

S.T.A.R. Labs is a research center in Metropolis.

Siobhan McDougal was the daughter of a powerful clan leader.

After her father's death, she tried taking over the clan but failed.

She was sent to live in the underworld.

Then one day, Siobhan met
an evil witch known as the Crone.
The witch promised to help her
return to the land of the living.

The Crone gave Siobhan superpowers and named her Silver Banshee.

In exchange for these gifts,

the witch asked for a magical old book.

It had belonged to Silver Banshee's father.

"Bring me the book," said the witch,

"or your powers will be lost."

Silver Banshee agreed to the task.

"Nothing will stop me!" she said.

Meanwhile, Clark Kent and Lois Lane reported on an event in Metropolis. An evil businessman named Lex Luthor was holding an auction of treasures.

Lex held up the final item for sale that day.

The crowd gasped at the rare book.

"Let's start the bidding at

one million dollars!" Lex said.

"Who would pay that price
for an old book?" Lois asked Clark.
But Clark wasn't listening.
His super-hearing had picked up
a strange sound outside.

SMASH! Silver Banshee suddenly
burst into the room.
"That book's not for sale," she shouted.
"It's mine!"

"This news story just

got interesting," said Lois.

She turned to Clark,

but he was nowhere to be found.

Out of sight, Clark shed his suit.

"This looks like a job

for Superman!" he said.

WHOOSH! The Man of Steel
soared back into the room.

"Give up!" Superman shouted
at Silver Banshee.

"Not until I've had the last word!"
said the angry villain.

Silver Banshee let loose
a sonic scream.

Her magic powers stopped
Superman in midair.

As Superman regained his strength, Silver Banshee returned to her evil task. "Where is it?" the villain shouted. Lex and the book were already gone!

"After I find that book, Superman, I'm coming back for you!" shouted Silver Banshee.

The villain fled into the night.

"My powers are useless

against magic," said Superman.

He flew toward S.T.A.R. Labs.

The research center built

tools to help super heroes.

"I have just the thing, Superman!"

said the lab's lead scientist.

He gave the hero a high-tech collar.

"If you put it on Silver Banshee

it will silence her scream,"

said the man.

Moments later, Superman arrived

in downtown Metropolis.

Silver Banshee was attacking

the LexCorp building.

She blasted the windows

with her sonic scream.

"Help, Superman!" Lex called out.

The evil businessman was trapped.

Superman was his only hope.

"I need to get close without
getting a splitting headache,"
said the Man of Steel.
He picked up a lead pipe
and broke it in half.

Superman molded the pieces
into tiny lead earplugs!
Silver Banshee spotted Superman.
"Didn't you learn your lesson
the first time?" she asked.

Silver Banshee opened her mouth.

SKREEEEEEEEEEEEEEE!

Sound waves exploded into the air.

But they did nothing to the hero.

Superman used his heat vision.
The blazing hot beams knocked
Silver Banshee down.

"Try this on for size!" said Superman.

He placed the collar around her neck.

Silver Banshee pulled and pulled,

but the device was locked tight.

"It's no use!" said the Man of Steel.

"Even your magic can't break it."

Superman smiled.

"Well," he said, "any last words?"

Silver Banshee opened her mouth.

This time, the high-tech collar

kept her scream from escaping.

The evil power filled inside her

like a balloon about to burst.

The device turned

Silver Banshee's magic against her.

BOOOOM!

She blasted back to

the underworld!

Superman then soared toward Lex

and grabbed the book from him.

"You'll pay for that!" Lex shouted.

"Consider us even," Superman said

as he flew off to hide the book from evil.